A Summer Full of Fireflies

Puppet

The door opened to the sound of footsteps
    knocking on the floor
He entered the room like the devil
Even the air dissected itself and
    prepared a path for him
All fell into puddles on the floor as he passed
She resisted while he came nearer
Her eyes never left his

They couldn't
    lest she fall

He entered her space and the defiance that
    held her upright so much longer than
    any of the others could no longer do so

She fell limp

Nearly reaching the floor before his arms
    caught her

Leaning in
> he placed hungry lips upon those he had
> secretly starved for under
> a facade of invulnerability

And to this her limbs wrapped around him and
> her mouth fed from a kiss that was
> like no other

As if somehow life had been breathed into
> a puppet

Alchemy

The respirations from his lungs slowed and
    he placed a hungry tongue
    between her open legs
He wanted to taste
    to savor the alchemy of their affections
Much like a honeybee at an open blossom
    in the early hours of morning
Enjoying the flavor brought about by the
    mixture of nectar and dewdrops

Burn

Raised hairs and a rapid pulse
    raged through her like wildfire
His mind was ablaze and his fingers like
    matchsticks
She had no choice
Allowing him to bind wrists and feet
    to the plush hearth beneath her
All she could do was lay there
Lay there and burn

Just for Her

The stars in the night sky
    twinkled before our eyes
Anyone could see them but
    they were shining just for her

In This Gallery

She sat and admired combinations of
    brushstrokes and paint that assembled
    gorgeous works residing on the walls
    around her
Unknowing that to him
She was far more priceless than any piece
    hanging in this gallery

A Welcoming

She had a love for the night sky
Adoration for the sparkle of starlight
Her heart developed an infatuation
    with the way the moon peeked through
    the wind driven cloud cover
So much so
    that she would lay in the grass on
    summer nights
Sliding her hand under a hiked up sundress and
    gliding fingers under dampened panties
    while dreaming of being taken
    by the night air as
    fireflies danced around her
Bathing her aroused being in a soft
    chartreuse glow
A welcoming by Asteria herself

Thirsty

My kisses landed on her skin like rain
    on the desert sand
She came
    to life and hair stood on end
A sacred oasis filled and I was invited to
    drench and refresh myself within
For I
    as well
    was ever so thirsty

Fire and Starlight

Stars were plucked from the night sky
    one by one
She used each to bring the wick of
    a single candle to flame
Placing the tiny fires throughout the room
    until the mixture of
    fire and starlight
    satisfied her eyes
She disrobed and bathed in the flickering light
    that was the perfect balance between
    Heaven and Hell
Her skin glowing and the flash of
    a sparkle in her eyes became a light
    he could no longer ignore
She took hold of his hands and drifted down
    to the bedding he had placed
    on the floor
There she drowned in
    the touch of his hands
    the comfort in his voice and
    the gaze of his starving eyes

He became the flame and she melted into
 a puddle of hot wax that his fingers
 couldn't keep themselves from
 dipping into

Eager to Taste

His face approached as she parted
    awaiting lips
Licking them first with a thirsty tongue
Eager to taste the rain she couldn't contain
    while he was kissing her elsewhere

Daffodils

My teeth and lips decorated the skin
    of her neck
Much the same as thunderstorms and sunlight
    bring springtime daffodils into bloom

Lullaby

A sigh

Eyes closing as fingers deeply
        searched through her hair
The nails scratching at her scalp
        played a song only she could hear
Notes sounded within as his lips kissed
        the back of her neck
A piece of flesh exposed by lifting the hair
        his hands were buried in
A strange cocktail of relaxation and arousal
        poured over her
Almost as if she were standing under
        a warm shower
Somehow she dreamed while still awake and
        this touch forced
        a longing to be wrapped in sheets
        and in his arms
More so than any lullaby sung from a parent
        to a child ever could

Tithes

I worshipped her like no goddess before
She required my tithes nightly
      sometimes to feed her
      some to adorn her holy face
      and others to be deposited in places
      only we would speak of
Places that could only be described as heaven
I devoutly paid in exchange for salvation

She Wore Red

She wore red so beautifully
The contrast between crimson and
    her complexion was
    something to behold
He adored the hue on her
    so wholeheartedly that
    his hands insisted the red remain
    on her skin
Even after the last stitch of her clothing had
    fallen to the floor

Moonlit

Our hands interlocked and moonlit
Lady Luna pouring light over my lover
    in a way the sun never could
We didn't speak
The vocabulary our eyes conversed with
    was all the dialogue necessary
Bringing her hand to my mouth allowed
    for the placement of a kiss
A kiss which lasted an immeasurable
    amount of time
The bony knuckle of her forefinger
    evenly distributed between my lips
I closed my eyes and wished that this moment
    would never end

Endured

The linens were soft and fresh
    against her skin
She lay comfortably with her legs draped over
    the side of the bed and turned her head to
    smile at her lover
The sheets were so cool against the
    side of her face

He approached

Strong hands lifted her ankles before
    parting and kneeling
    between them
His lips kissed the outer and his tongue tasted
    the insides of her body
As he did a warm breeze entered the room
    from the open window
    at his back
The scent of lilacs swirled and mixed with
    the aroma of the ever dampening
    woman under his nose
He breathed and as his lungs exhaled
    a moan softly traveled from his mouth
    onto and into the flesh he was
    probing
    and
    tasting

This was the spring he had endured winter for

First Spring Storm

The smile her lips curved into
    and
    the voice with which she spoke
Stirred my soul like the lightning and thunder
    from the first spring storm

So Like a Rose

So like a rose
Pink petals were admired by adoring eyes
      as he brought this bloom
      close enough to
      inhale her fragrance
Kisses were softly laid upon her as fingers and
      a firm yet gentle tongue
      opened her farther than
      she ever would have for sunlight
Even on the warmest of summer days

Passport

As he called out and spilled over the grip
    her hand held upon his
    glistening
    saliva coated flesh
She took him to a place no passport would
    ever grant a traveler access

Apothecary

There were bottles marked with single letters

"H"

"M"

"V"

"A"

She lay on the sheets as my apothecary
Ready to prescribe anything that would
      calm what ailed me

Afterwards

She loved touching herself
      when her love was away
The way her body felt against
      its own grip
A dull world disappearing as fingers
      pushed
      turned and
      lifted before being
      plunged into her warmth
Afterwards
      at the times she felt
      exceptionally devilish
Hers sent his phone photographs of
      glistening hands
Only to torture him in the hours it would be
      before he could return home

Strange World

Of all the planets and places he could
 choose to explore
Only hers was a world strange enough to
 conquer his curiosity

Map

Fingernails dug in and traced along her skin
Leaving a pink scratch that was reminiscent
    of a winding line on a
    faded piece of paper
    leading the way to buried gold
A map was never necessary as he knew places
    under her flesh
    where treasure was always found
A find more valuable than any chest of
    coins
    jewels or
    stones

Spinning the Globe

I used to love spinning the globe and blindly
    stopping it with my finger
Pretending where I placed fingerprints was
    a place I would someday visit
Now the childish game holds no merit
Because where I prefer to go is any place
    she can be found at my side

Fireplace

There is no place for those who have
    given everything
    to keep loved ones warm than
    among the ashes in the fireplace
    of a loving home

Catching the Rain

Palms upward towards the thundercloud
    of a man
    that she called her lover
How she loved closing her eyes during storms
    smiling and
    catching the warm summer rain
    in her hands

Wax Seal

Unusually soft and slow

Thinking as though she could feel
      each space between his fingerprints as he
      turned
      lifted and
      rotated her epicenter
Attempts to feel even more and push against him
      were cut short by firm grips
      delivered by a free hand
      that held her still

A stark contrast to the
      tender turning touch between
      shaking
      open legs

He continued until she came

A controlled flow saturated with tension
      left her
As he continued to finish her using the care
      of one placing a wax seal
      on a love letter

Voyage

The moonlight falling across her skin
    gave itself
    back to my eyes countless times
She lay so still
Wrapped in sweat and accented by the
    lust of mine she was determined
    to bring upon her chest
The rise and fall of her breathing
    sparkled in my sight like patient waves
Reflecting the moon as the tide drew them
    away from the shore

How I wanted to float away with them

I lay upon her once more
Our skin meeting the way ocean swells
    dance against the cool night air
And far beyond the sight of any life
    watching from the sand
Lips and tongues meet
Creating islands and bringing about
    new places to rest
        during any voyage across the sea

Not the One

"Take it off."
"What are you talking about?"
"The makeup."
"Why?"
"I want you to suck me and fuck me with
     the beautiful face you were born with.
     Not the one you wish you had."

Only Love

The petals were pulled
    one by one
She began with "He loves me."
    and
       continued with "He loves me."
Never once using "He loves me, not."

Because it simply wasn't true

This flower represented him and it was
    only love

The Golden Hour

We walked through the cobblestone streets
    hand in hand
Fingers intertwined in the same fashion the
    warm light of the golden hour
    found its way into the shadows
    between the bricks
Sometimes the surface was uneven
We held onto each other to make the stroll
    a little easier
The sun slowly set and the air turned cool
The hearts in our chests remained warm
Connected by touch in the hands that we held
    and in soul by the silent moment
    we were surrounded by

Thoughts of Winter

When he held her the air was never cold
It was warm like
    sunlight
Bright like a summer day
Her skin became hot to the touch
    and thoughts of winter
      melted away

For His Eyes Only

She didn't look into the mirrors she passed
    while her skin was covered
    by lace
Vanity or self judgement wasn't to be
    her focus

She knew he loved it and
    she loved that a different flavor of
    adoration washed over his expression
    whenever she dressed this way

And after all of the things he had given to her
    this was a gift
    for his eyes only

How to Look

Looking down hadn't ever given her
    much joy
In her eyes the view of flowers she was
    once adorned with
    had long been replaced
    by unsightly branches filled by
    leaves that allowed her survival and
    a new generation to be
His eyes saw something hers couldn't
From where he stood the stems and twigs
    still held so many beautiful blooms
He knew how to look to see them
    and how lucky his retinas were
    to be gifted the vision of her blossoms
    swaying in the warm spring breeze

Scent of Home

Spring
    is full of the aroma of
    raindrops and flowers

Summer of
    sunscreen and
    mowed grass

Autumn winds carry
    harvested fields and
    fallen leaves

    while

Winter's dry air fills my nose with
    cocoa on snowy days and the
    red cedar burning in the fireplace

When my arms wrap around her
    no matter the season
The skin where her neck meets her shoulders
    carries the scent of home

Bruised Fruit

Perfection didn't catch his eye
The damaged could easily be enjoyed
    every bit as much as
    those who had never
    fallen from the branch to the ground
He always had a taste for the
    soft sweetness of
    bruised fruit

Knot

We were a knot so tight
    it couldn't be untied
No matter who tugged at each end

Nurtured

Sheets became the wind that wrapped
    around us
Our limbs entangled like an entire forest
    had just fallen
While the sweat from skin
    and the trickles of our enamoration
    that fell from within her
    nurtured the soil that was the mattress
    on which we slept

A Closer Look

A late summer darkness consumed the sky
    as the constellations came out
    of hiding
She lay him back on the warmth radiating
    from the concrete of the patio
Her hand found his pants and began to
    unzip them at a painfully slow pace
    as he strained and pushed against
    the fabric she was opening
Once released
    she brought lips to meet him before
    taking him deeply into her mouth
Both becoming wetter each time her face
    met the jeans he was standing through
Upon letting him go
    she remarked how beautiful
    his vein-heavy form looked
    shimmering in the moonlight

Then she straddled him
    speaking of how convenient it was
    that she had not been wearing panties
    under her sundress
She grinned a smile that may very well have
    only existed to her as she repeatedly
    took him at length
Her knees scuffing themselves
    against the pavement eventually
    bringing the sting of broken skin
    as he began to tense inside of her
Another smile graced her face as the groans
    she was determined to hear
    made their way
    past his lips
All while the stars in the night sky above them
    began to fall
    one after another
Literally dying to get a closer look

Like a Bell

He made her sing and
    chime like a bell
All while soon to be disappointed angels
    waited for wings that would never appear

July Girl

If there were words to describe her
She was a July girl who lived for
    summer rain
    rainbows and the
    thunder and lightning that divided them

Summer Afternoons

She stood in front of the window
    casting the shadow of her naked form
    towards me
The dark
    distorted and
    lengthy manifestation
    nearly reached to where I sat
    waiting patiently for her
She walked towards me
Slowly
Taking as long to reach me as it did for
    the sun to find itself low in the
    near evening sky

...or so it seemed

I tasted her warm
    sunlight-kissed skin as hands
    began to wander through my hair
This being how summer afternoons were
    intended to be spent by the
    entity who created them

Make a Wish

One hand with a white knuckle grip on her hip
The second pushed into the dip of a
    beautifully arched back
Amid the delightful turmoil
    she turned to look over her shoulder
    and catch a glimpse of him
She was bent over like a dandelion being
    pushed by a warm summer breeze
And he was ready to blow and
    make a wish

Opals & Wood Grain

Droplets formed across her
An indication of the energy she used
    when fucking me
Much as opals and wood grain
    appear so much more vivid when wet
So did her soul glow when she
    shimmered with sweat and
        the liquid she forced my body to spray
        across her skin

Burst

The book stayed in her frail hands
Eyes watched through the window to
    ensure she was alone
As the house grew silent
    she pulled up her dress
    and began exploring the tender skin
    veiled by thin panties
    with curious fingers
Deafening was the sound brought by
    the combination of her lungs exhaling
    and the book she held falling to and
    striking the hardwood floor
So much louder than any thunder from
    a nearby lightning strike could be
She wanted to believe it was the startle
    that brought the tiny burst of fluid
    to dampen the fabric
    between folds of flesh and fingertips

Ladybug

We sat in the grass enjoying the warm
    summer breezes that
    whispered in our ears
Protected from the sunlight by the shadows cast
    from the mature trees we relaxed under
Hands were held and kisses exchanged
    when a tickle drew my attention
I raised my hand and watched a diligent ladybug
    ascend my arm
She climbed steadily through the hair
    on my wrist before
    standing on my fingertip and
    flying away

No words were spoken

Just smiles growing from the assumption
    that we were both wishing for the wind to
    carry us away

Fluent

It wasn't always easy for him to express
      thoughts and feelings through words
But in the languages of
      eye contact
      kiss and
      touch
In those
      he was more than fluent

Bloomed at Night

She was a strange little flower that only
    bloomed at night
When the moon was high her petals would open
    so she could feed upon its light
She twirled and danced
    skipped and pranced
    wherever the light had shown
As in love by herself as a blossom could be
At times
    she hated to dance all alone

Ready to Forsake

The angels watched
Congregating in secret
Transfixed by the sight of her legs being
    lifted so high
Her feet held together by a mere man she all but
    swore was divine himself
They spoke amongst themselves
Ready to forsake a life in the clouds
    for a chance to experience
    everything she was feeling
Merely a glimpse of this new
    more indulgent form of heaven
    left them starving
It had never been in their hearts
    to leave their god
    to lose their wings
    until now

Perseid

Leaving the pavement to stop on a
    small patch of gravel
A little place just off
    Flint Bottom Road where
    so many late summer nights were spent
    watching the Perseid meteors fall
We used the fading evening sunlight to gaze
    into one another's eyes
Between her soft kisses and
    enthusiastic whimpers
    I become aware that one of
    the countless wishes I had made under
    the falling stars of August
    was right next to me
Warmly wrapped around my fingers

Celestial

She wasn't my star
    my sun or
    my moon
She was my entire fucking sky

Can't See a Thing

My bare skin joined hers under
    fresh
    cool
    sheets
I paused to place my glasses on the nightstand
    next to the bed
I can't see a thing without them but this
    never distracted me from my path
I knew my way by heart

Comfort

Cum for me because it comforts me

Everything I Needed

The room was dark and I was
>unable to see
>unable to read her expressions

But the way her throat cried out
>while her body undulated at the
>mercy of my hands
>>told me everything I needed to know

Word for Word

Fingertips indented flesh as he
     opened her with force and
     deliberation
She was spread farther than her mind
     had ever thought of allowing its body to be

He ravaged her

Tearing through her contents
     page to page
     and from cover to cover
His actions left her sore
     in both body and mind
Some would say "damaged"
     but she preferred "changed"

Her binding now broken and uneven

A welcomed alteration
As she now had no inclination to ever
     spend time resting on a shelf
No desire to stand next to the straight spines
     of books who were never opened
     and read word for word

To Be Felt

She didn't only want to be touched
She wanted to be felt

Between Pages

Petals and leaves were placed between
    her favorite pages
She wanted to gift something beautiful
    to the printed words
    that had given themselves to her
    and
    unknowingly brought her so much joy

A Simple Bouquet

There are thousands of wishes in any
    field of dandelions
I would need but a simple bouquet

All But Grass

They laid and loved in a
        secluded meadow on
        a hot summer day
Nothing touched enamored ears except for
        their breathing
        their voices
            the sound of their love as it interrupted
            the whispering of the world around them
And in the years after one couldn't keep
        the flowers from blooming
Where for centuries this place was barren to
        all but grass

Healing

Vibrant colors flashed under my
    closed eyelids
Quaking and shuddering as she
    swallowed and
    continued to suck
The bliss that permeated my soul
    couldn't be referred to as an orgasm
It could only be described as healing

Sustenance

Upon finishing
His hand held and
      gently lifted her chin
Letting her know to make eye contact
      before she swallowed
A smile appeared as she gazed at her
      heavily breathing lover's
      flush and blotchy cheeks

She dashed his release down her throat

Gaining a seemingly minute
      amount of nourishment
      for her body from what he gave
Insignificant
      at least in comparison to the
      sustenance her soul received
      while extracting it

Playing With Fire

There was no doubt
She knew what she was doing
Lessons had been learned on previous nights
    but these actions seemed to
    contradict their wisdom

Completely aware she was playing with fire

The risk of being burned paled in comparison
    to the pain of being apart from a spark
    and
        not feeling the heat of her lover's affection

Smoke

She moved and turned like
    cigarette smoke and I couldn't look away
I knew that she was
    cancerous
    deadly and
    dangerous
But I breathed so deeply anyway

I was held in a space by the grace of
    her face like she was comprised of nicotine
Inhaling only once had me
    addicted
    devoted
    restricted
Like nothing I had ever seen

Renaissance

The panties she wanted him to see
    slid down the fair skin of her
    beautiful legs
Resembling the final brushstroke of an artist
    completing their masterpiece
A true renaissance was about to begin

On the Page

Sweat
    saliva and
    the liquid of our lust was strewn
    across the sheets like
    poetry on the page

Balance

The violence in his desire
The sweetness in his love
She had a need for both
    the pain from bruises and welts
Alongside the warmth of
    the most tender kisses and cuddles
It was all about the balance in an understanding
    none had shown before

Decorate

The only reason she was given skin was
for him to decorate it

Sunday Morning

The unmistakable aroma and
    subsequent anticipation of
    that first sip
When the warmth held in hands
    touched early morning lips
    she smiled
The first swallow warmed her soul like the
    taste of coffee
    on a chilly Sunday morning
Waking and alerting her senses to the sound of
    this lover's labored breathing

Hymnal

The organ played as she stood
    on an early morning
    wearing her simple
    Sunday dress
Hands opening up the hymnal
    before resting it against her breasts
Smiling to herself as she gently pushed its covers
    to tease hidden nipples that
    were sensitive and sore
The binding resting between them and
    across from skin his liquid had flown over
    the night before
Her voice weary from the delightful agony
    she expressed while he was
    filling her space
Certain notes were masked in rasp
    but she carried on with amazing grace

Distraction

Legs crossed under her
      as she took a seat at the opposite end
      of the couch
      and covered her lap with the
      blanket that was kept there
He looked
      before smiling as a greeting before
      returning his eyes to the
      television program he was so
      intently watching
When she noticed his attention drift from her
      she easily slid her fingers underneath
      the pajama bottoms she wore
Turning and pushing
Trying to keep still and quiet
      became more difficult as she felt
      the familiar swell rising from within
The tiniest gasp caught his ear
Causing him to turn and notice her rosy cheeks
      and a sly
      adorable smile

He didn't need to ask
He just quietly reached for the remote
    turned off the television
        and leaned towards her to taste the
        outstretched hand she offered

See Her Shine

She thrived in the darkness
      because
In the light no one could see her shine

On Fire

Crawling under cool evening sheets
Covered hands tucked the comforter
    tightly under her chin before speaking
    and
    letting me know that she was freezing
I had no choice but to snuggle in closer
    slide my hand up from her knee
    into the shorts
    and
    panties she wore to bed
    and
    proceed in setting her on fire

Maples and Oaks

They ducked away into a small space that
    no one
    not even the sun could see
Giggling and kissing while his wandering hands
    found their way past
    the button of her jeans and
    the elastic of her panties
His left below her stomach and
    his right under her back

A finger from each found its way and alternated
    between entering and exiting
Dancing with each other in the same slick space

Her knees buckled to accommodate his touch
Eventually shaking and finding trouble
    holding her upright
She repeatedly splashed against his grip as
    his teeth chewed at the neck that
    seemed to be dropping
    lower and lower

Knees eventually struck the ground before she
     began clawing at the front
     of his pants
She pulled him out
     placed his hands in her hair

"Please hurry."
She said desperately before starting to suck

Fingers dug into her scalp as he fucked her face
     without restraint
At times she gagged
     eyes watering
     but she couldn't
     and wouldn't
     allow this to stop

His legs shuddered as she clamped her lips
     tightly and
     swallowed her prize

His feet and her knees becoming roots
     that would forever nurture memories
     of the lust they had lived
     under the shade of the maples and oaks

Naked

Watching every moment as she undressed
> in front of him

Timid fingers slightly shaking and fumbling with
> buttons
> zippers and
> clasps

His eyes adored hers
Knowing that while she took so much time
> exposing her skin

She was also baring her soul
And in doing so becoming more naked than she
> ever cared to be in front of anyone
> other than the lover who reached out to
> touch and
> feel anything she would allow

Dancing

Though laying down with the back of her head
    enjoying the pillows evening coolness
I loved to keep her dancing on the
    tip of my tongue

New Life

The burning felt by our hearts
    when ignited for the one we love
Sets the world ablaze like a forest fire
    clearing a path for new life to grow

Blue

When my eyes turned upwards
    I only saw blue
But when my irises met with hers
    I could finally see the sky

Curtsy

September fades into October
    as the leaves change hue
They blow in the breeze as a woman
    wearing a new dress
    in the sight of her lover
Twirling and turning
Flirting and teasing her autumnal admirer
Greeting him with a smile and
    bestowing a curtsy
    as he bowed his head
Eventually falling to her knees and
    scattering the foliage of her skirt
    among the grass

Playlist

An endless sky
Days of freedom from the requirements of
    employment
A long road to travel
An even longer playlist ready to
    accept the challenge
    and
        a hand to hold throughout the journey

Masks

Though being windows to the soul
    I long for more than eyes
I miss the faces
I miss the smiles
I miss the humanity in the expressions from my
    brothers and sisters as they cross my path
The simplest of things this pandemic
    and its masks
    has robbed from me

Around the Sun

The warmth of spring and the
    brightness of summer
    will be but a memory
Autumn will fade into winter
    when snowflakes fall
        to fill the bottom half of the hourglass
        that was this tumultuous trip
    around the sun

After All

Her laughter was joy and
      her smile was bright
She could bring blue to the cloudiest of skies

But her heart after all
      was quite broken and small
Tears locked within the blinks of her eyes

There Was Rain

Even the sunshine that illuminated her eyes
    became tired
They darkened
They clouded
And on the hardest of days there was rain

Decipher

The umbrellas were left closed and standing
    where they were stored
It was time to walk among the others with
    cheeks that couldn't decipher between
    the droplets falling from the sky
    and those that had been dropping
    from her eyes

Salty and Familiar

Fingertips pushed through her hair
    until I felt the firm skin
    of her scalp
The tears rolling from wobbling eyes
    coated my lips
    when I used kisses to catch them
I tasted her pain
    salty
    and
    familiar
But at the same time
    nothing like mine

Weight

The weight of her fruit can become
    too much to bear
Her beautiful branches droop and sag
    toward soil that has been
    irrigated and softened by her tears
The threat of those branches being torn and
    ripped from her trunk
    keeps me trying to help support them
    day after day
Waiting for the time her fruit is harvested to be
    loved by others in addition to her
    so that her crown might reach for the
    sunshine above us
Afraid that I, myself can't stand and
    hold her up forever
Despite the love and best intentions in my heart

Slow Motion

When she smiles at me
When she laughs
My eyes watch it happen in slow motion
  as these moments are cherished and few
  when compared to the times I see her
  only being strong because she feels
  there is no other choice

Day After Day

Sometimes
Sometimes when I'm alone I cry
I cry for her
I cry for myself
I cry for what I hoped could be
I cry because loving her means
    watching her in pain
    day after day
I see the tears fall and watch the muscle relaxers
    being taken
I read the sending of "thoughts and prayers"
    while what would bring true relief
    is unspoken by those who never truly
    witness her toil
    but whose voices she needs to hear
The transition from parent to caretaker
    is complete and undeniable
    but her loving heart sees no difference
She is admirable but weak
All I can do is watch

Watch the woman I love
    trapped
    isolated and
    in pain
I truly enjoy lightening her weight
    but it can never be enough
I will stay alongside my love
I will watch life unfold and witness her
    blossom or break
    and I have so much fear of the latter
I will stand with her and thrive or crumble
    hand in hand
    over the time it takes
I will be here to see and listen to what
    no one else does
Because I love her
    and that's what lovers do

Ashes as Snowflakes

The love I have for her burns with a heat greater
    than any sun
So warm that the ashes float from the flames
    and fall to the earth as snowflakes

Nightmare

Mumbles
Whispers
Erratic and restless movements
Fragments of words from what her lips
    may have been saying
    on the other side of consciousness
I moved in close
Kissed her shoulder and
    laid my hand on the center of her chest
    in an effort to calm her
    rapidly pounding heart
What I wouldn't give to enter her mind
    bring my love peace and
    return this nightmare to a dream

Distance

You're right here when my eyes can see
In my bed and
        in my hands
But even when I hold you
You feel so far away

Hidden Places

There are so many
    quiet
    lonely
    hidden places
    scattered throughout my mind
Places I want to be with you

If Only

If only the rain would fall
    to hide these tears
Constant thunder
    to cover the sound of my cries
Lightning
    to blind and distract any eyes from the
    expression of my broken heart

No Quiet

There is no quiet anymore
No silence to accompany
      hours spent alone
The stillness would always aid in the
      purging of anxiety and stress
Now this mute elixir only exists in memory
So much so that even the
      noiselessness of the overnight hours
      have fallen prey to potential
      chaos
      worry and
      pain
No reticent moment is safe

Going Forward

Moving on is hard and
    going forward seems impossible
Fog and raindrops hit the windshield
Making the recurrence of those memories
    absolutely unstoppable

Heartbeat

The emotion is always there
The pain never leaves because the heart is
    eternally hopeful
Unknowingly force feeding those
    beautiful memories to your soul
    every time it beats

Stars at Twilight

I would love to embrace the evening sun
    as she sets
I want to burn and disappear
    with the daylight
To witness the emergence of twinkling
    stars at twilight
But have them unable to see me

Identifiable

What we're really looking for is
    someone who doesn't necessarily
    love us the same way
    but
Someone who loves with an identifiable ferocity
A desire to sacrifice
    to compromise
    to make you just as happy as
    you wish you could make them

Us

In dreams she chose me the way I do
    when my eyes are open
It was her
    with me
    we
Our souls there to embrace one another
    in any moment
    needed of each other
Hearts drinking from the same glass
    in the same time
    in the same frame of mind
Not completely our own

We were us

The Sill

I can see it
A life out there - bright and warm
Self doubt and heartache act like glass
    and I am the housefly repeatedly
    running into the window
Eventually joining my stiffened
    brothers and sisters
    who have gathered on
    the sill down below

Axes

Branches and foliage may reach for the sky
    to bask in the warmth of the sun and
    gaze at the way stars wink and twinkle
    at one another
    on the clearest of summer nights
But my roots
My roots stay in the ground
Dark
Damp and
Lonely in their existence
All for onlookers to appreciate the shade of
    something beautiful and full
A structure supported by
    hurt and
    dirt
A place to stand while saws growl and axes swing

Self Abuse

I've always felt that you are built of the
    decisions you choose
Why does opting to be the bigger person and
    a good man feel like self abuse

Rescue Me

So many parts of me were
      drowning
More pieces than even a god could ever save
I stand tiptoed with my wrist
      breaching the surface
With nothing racing through my mind
      but the thought of ways
      to have better utilized
      that last breath

The only one that seems to matter

And a hope in this panicked heart that
      my deity would reach her hand down and
      rescue me

Crickets

When the frost arrives
    I hang my head
The new silence in
    sunless hours of morning greets me
    with a fragility so much colder than that
    of the air
As the leaves and crickets were the only things
    that seemed to applaud my existence
It becomes so difficult to see spring
    on the horizon
When the dead of winter knocks at your door

Watch the Sky

When darkness falls
    and the air turns cool
Lift the chin from your chest
Turning your eyes to the
    unlit air above you
Peer through the scattering of fireflies
Focus on the stars glimmering against the pitch
    and
        watch the sky for me

Crumbled

Even if the moon crumbled and
    fell from the sky
I would be here to hold you while the oceans
    swelled and greedily took the earth
    as their own
My arms would wrap around
    holding you against me
Trying to keep your body still as you
    thrashed about
    with a pounding heart desperately
    waiting for that next breath

One that never comes

All before the moment arrives
    when I would weaken and let go
    so we could drift and settle on the ground
    we used to walk hand in hand upon
Catching a wavy view of the stars that seemed to
    shine ever so brightly
    in the absence of lunar light

World of Two

All I want is to walk
To take strides hand in hand through the
    warm summer sunshine
Talking and engaging in
    spontaneous
        uninterrupted conversation
Occasionally stopping for momentary embraces
    and the salty kisses that result
        from July's humid air

When home we could shower together
Smiling
Giggling and
Growling when soapy fingers were allowed to
    slide into places not as often explored

We'd dry and I would make us dinner
Anxiously watching your eyes as you take those
    first few bites
    and being relieved when
    eyebrows lift before you look my way
    and smile

After dinner our bodies retire to the sofa with
    post-meal drinks in hand

A film playing on the screen while our skin
    becomes distracted
The action being displayed by light and sound
    going unnoticed and ignored

Bedtime comes with
    blankets
    kisses and
    silent thoughts of the world we've built
    together

This beautiful world of two

My Tomorrow

On this knee and
      with this ring
I ask you to join me in life
To lay our pasts to burn on the bridges
      that lead the way to
      a world we build for each other
I offer you this heart
And in doing so I promise to
      treasure you
      support you and
      be there when you need me
Will you be my tomorrow?
Because I would love to be your every day

So Many Fireflies

The lights from so many fireflies
    reflected back over the blue of her eyes
A similar sparkle hadn't been in view
    since the first time they blinked after
    hearing me say "I love you."

Vintage

They had a strange
    almost vintage type of love
Doors were held open
    flowers were sent
    fingers were intertwined on
    restaurant tables
Courtesies thought long lost to recent times
    were alive and well throughout their days
But the nights
The nights were filled with acts one would prefer
    be deleted from their browser history

Visitor

Warm summer sunshine covered everything
Gently burning the back of her neck
    as she sat
Watching the honeybees
    feed from and pollinate the flowers
    she had planted
    brought so much joy
Blood rushed and breath was held as
    a nearly weightless visitor landed on
    her bare knee
Walking across her skin for several
    uncounted seconds
    before taking flight and returning to work
The tiny rush of air pushed by minuscule wings
    was the only goodbye that
    seemed necessary
She smiled and took this visit as a sign that
    the lover her thoughts couldn't
    save themselves from
    was thinking about her, too

New Year's Day

All was not quiet on New Year's Day
The room became light and
    my hands had awoken hungry
My grip feasted on gorgeous
    thighs and buttocks
Spreading her open and occasionally
    tracing soft circles over her ass
    with my fingertips

Moving forward I discovered she was thoroughly
    warm
    wet and
    inviting

I moved to support myself on still sleepy knees

Lifting her feet
    I kissed on their soles after pushing my
    tongue between adorable little toes
Her legs were then held and
    allowed to rest at my chest

I found and easily sank into her as an
        indiscernible expletive
        was gasped from her lips

There happened to be no snow
        covering the ground on this
        January morning
However I would be providing plenty of white

A Deep Breath

Knees and sheets
Elbows to the mattress as feet hung from the
    edge of the bed
Naked and exposed
Feeling the wind he created from
    what she assumed was the
    removal of clothing
    brush over skin not so akin to
    breathing such fresh air
A single hand slid down her spine before both
    gripped and slightly held her open
    as she took a deep breath
    closed her eyes and
    let it happen

Stitches

Remaining focused proved so difficult
The memories of what she had done
The way her mouth made me feel
The skin on which she'd placed that tongue
    and those kisses
Attempting to restrain those thoughts from
    entering my mind
    was harder than
    holding still and
    keeping my hands from
    scratching at stitches

Suffering

This
Her
This was the taste that took
    the suffering away
The flavor that pulled
    the stars out of the sky

Gifting him a darkness to truly shine in

A lavender light she could only see
    when her eyes were closed the tightest

Melody

I couldn't remember the things I had
      seen or heard in my sleep
As much as I tried
      there was a veil of nothingness
      separating these thoughts from
      my daylight mind
When looking at her I could almost recall
      but never quite grasp
Maybe the melody of how we loved together
      in a world of our own
        was one I could only hear in my dreams

A New Gravity

A new gravity took hold of her
Dragging the body she thought she owned
    back and keeping it still
      against her will

The first steps he took into the room
    weren't audible
They grew with intensity as he came closer
    until the sounds from his stride
    were all that she could hear

At times it was as if even the breath he exhaled
    seemed to scream into her ears

She was pinned
    trapped and
    held in place with the invisible chains of
    his presence
Everything faded to black and every noise heard
    drifted away into silence

Only to become
    blinding white and
    deafening
    when his lips touched hers

Reverberation

When his hand met her ass
        there was such an intense
        reverberation
Not in the room or
        in her ears
Through her body
Through her soul
The marks he left were deep and red
        like the words of Christ
This is how she wanted to be saved

Undergarment

She was never without an undergarment
    covering the ass he loved to handle
On days without panties she wore
    the memories he left as handprints

Neither of Us

"Neither of us will be left unfulfilled.
    Understand?"

Her only response was an enthusiastic nod
    as his hands held her neck with
    such a grip that it was
    impossible for her to speak
She breathed deeply and childishly smiled
    the moment he let go
    took a single step back and
    began to loosen his belt

Pillar of Salt

At times he was afraid to look
    directly at her
Surely gazing upon this divinity and
    the beautiful destruction she was bringing
    would turn him into a pillar of salt

Web

Pinpoints of brightness allowed themselves to
    highlight the curves of her bare chest

Beads of sweat covered her
    some from her
    others were mine
A familiar smile and
    exhausted eyes dressed her face
    in opulence

She lay there

Each wrist tied to its corresponding bed post
    while I stood in awe
Admiring her beauty as the skin I gazed upon
    rose and fell from her labored breathing
She was draped across the place we slept
    like a spider's web
One decorated with dewdrops and
    glowing in the light that poured from the
    early morning sun

Composing myself I stepped toward her

Extending an arm and using my hands
    one on her
    and the other on myself

She tried to remain quiet but
      the tiny bursts against my internal coaxing
      along with the undeniable firmness
      my fingers found in their grasp
Let us both know that it was time for her
      to once again be the butterfly
      entangled in the arachnid's snare

She wasn't going anywhere

So Often Spoke

The begging
The pleading before the act
Tasting her own pleasure all over his skin
    before stroking him with deliberation and
    sucking him with intent
She wanted his desire to fill her mouth
To swallow the bliss he felt with the tongue that
    cherished him so
The tongue that so often spoke the words
    "I love you."

Blades of Grass

My hands wrapped around her ankles tightly and
    lifted them high
I pushed them away from me
    folding these beautiful legs back
    toward her
My eyes wandered lower to watch as I repeatedly
    entered her body
My skin shimmering more with each
    passing second
Catching the sight of a blissful expression
    peeking from momentarily
    parted knees stirring memories of
    the morning sunlight
    shining through
    long
    tall
    blades of grass
Bringing another bright spring day to the
    both of us

Sunburn

I entered the room like the morning sun
Lifting the overnight fog and
    removing her clothing with
    my warm hands
Revealing the beautiful ground below
    and the fair skin that would soon be
    begging for me to make it burn

Blend

She was a blend of
      salty and sweet
      sacred and secular
      angelic and delightfully devilish
Dressed only in panties that were
      pulled to the side because I was
      too impatient to remove them

Collection of Souls

Strolling along concrete paths
Silently reciting
    the names and dates engraved upon
        the rows of vertical slabs to themselves
Occasionally bringing the other's attention to
    certain features that stood out on
    the more unique tablets of stone
Things included on the marker
    that granted the deceased more identity
    than simply who they were and
    how many years they had accumulated

Their walk had become horizontal as he
    dragged her down into the
    dry
    crumbling
    autumn leaves
Climbing atop he kissed and bit at her neck
    while she tried to
    breathe through the ticklish laughter
    she couldn't contain
She coyly looked around them as the buttons
    on her shirt were released
    one by one

Their rustling began to stir the spirits

The unseen gathered around them as he kissed
    her now bare chest and
    moved his hand down to
    unbutton her pants

Hands were held by lovers fortunate enough
    to have been buried together

Standing among them were also those who
    passed before
Only to lie alone and
    silently watch while their
    widows and widowers
    found love again
Eventually resting in peace somewhere
    alongside their subsequent lovers

None could
    but all felt as if they were smiling
Like they could somehow feel what these
    young lovers did
    as they pleased each other
    between the trees and headstones
Feelings some hadn't known for over
    a hundred years

The lovers dressed and walked hand in hand
    before exiting through the
    cemetery gates

Countless spirits became one as they
    crowded the entrance
Congregating between pillars
    that served as a threshold
    they were unable to cross

Wishing they could be seen or
    have voices heard as
    all were desperate to
    wish these visitors well and
    ask them to return again soon

A prismatic glow was cast on the concrete
    as the afternoon sun shone through
    this unusual collection of souls

The couple eventually meandered out of sight
    before the cluster began to disperse

Finding their forever homes and
    sightlessly glowing with
    the young love this day brought
Because too many only bring sadness and tears
    to the air above their resting places

Beneath the Surface

The evening air of midnight in August
    felt so cool to our saturated skin
Clothing lay upon the shore as we allowed
    the water of the lake to
    wrap herself around our naked bodies

My lover used greedy hands to make me
    harder than her nipples
    after we swam to one another
    met and
    kissed under the luminescence
    of a clear summer sky

The moon became enraged as the water mocked
    the satellite with her waving reflection
Taunting and childishly teasing the orbiting light
Filling her with envy as the rippled mirroring
    kept the greatest of details out of sight
    and
    hidden beneath the surface

Form of Flight

She didn't want to live where other angels
    called home
She need not have wings at her back while
    he was between her legs
This was indeed a heaven
And looking down to watch the expression
    on that face
        while he came inside of her
        was the only form of flight
        she ever cared to possess

Splinter

The memories of the way he loved were
    silent like a splinter
Coming to life and making their presence known
    when her skin was touched just right

Her Own Darkness

When she let go and
        embraced her own darkness
She could finally shine for him
But even more so
        could the light from underneath a
        lifted veil
        illuminate a path to an existence
        where they were the center of the universe
Others as mere planets rotating individually
        and circling the sun that blinded their eyes

Journeyman

His fingers and his hands
    turning
    twisting and
    pulling the jute
The urge to move was at times
    painfully undeniable but
    so was the light in his eyes as he worked
He was indeed an artisan
    a journeyman
A craftsman whose trade was taking her
    mobility away
The anticipation of being delightfully violated
    upon the completion of his task
    grew with each knot he tied
When close enough
    he could smell her desire
    but he continued to toil away
Transforming his limber love into a
    fixed sculpture
One with the neediest eyes his had ever been
    blessed with looking into

COVID

It was as though even her eyes smiled
    as I entered the room and
    tossed my jacket into the chair
    at my right
She stood
Naked from the waist down
    her feet slowly taking steps in my direction

"Protection?"
She shyly asked from across the room
    at a distance easily more than six feet
"One can't be too careful."

I smiled and nodded before speaking
"I've come prepared."

Leaning towards the chair I reached into
    body temperature coat pockets
    before placing the face mask and
    hand sanitizer I pulled from them
    on a nearby table

She laughed deeply as I displayed the condom
    that was hiding in my shirt pocket

It was time to throw any social distancing
    recommendations out the window

Carousel

The slow gradual fullness overtook her
      as she settled
      and took him fully
Palms were pushed into flesh covering
      the chest below her
This allowed for her beautiful body to
      lift
      descend
      rotate and
      rock against his
And as she did closed eyes granted her senses
      the pleasure of enjoying a
      carnival carousel
The hot summer air lifting her hair
      with its gentle breezes
      as she went up and down
And the spinning
How she loved the spinning

Stepping Stones

Fresh cotton
Laying upon her shoulders in a way that
    made his teeth jealous
A creased collar held itself
    around her neck as his hands did in
    daydreams
Buttons placed in tight keyhole shaped openings
    dropped down her chest
Plunging out of sight behind the waistline
    of her skirt
Providing stepping stones for the kisses
    he applied to each
    before the fasteners were
    undone by his expert fingers
    to reveal the most tasteful of
    brassieres
A garment whose obscuring cups he
    replaced with the cheeks she lightly
    kissed upon their first meeting

Cheeks that provided hundreds of pinpoints
    in the form of beard stubble
        that would force nipples to stand erect
        against the side of his face
Her shirt was untucked and the skirt
    dropped to the floor as her skin became
    completely exposed to the fluorescent light
    of the room
Putting her hand to his chest
    he fell back slightly
Stumbling onto to the floor and looking up
    slightly surprised
Her approach never wavered as he was forced
    onto his back to where she could
    rest with his head between her legs
There was no more room for small talk
It was time for business

She Knew

Whenever he was near or
    could possibly be watching
She made sure to always bend at the waist
    when picking items off the floor
Simply because she knew it drove him crazy

Sick

For days he had laid across the couch
    aching
    coughing and
    sick
She looked at him with such pity
Wishing he would suck up his "man cold"
    long enough to bend her over
    and give up some dick

Congregation

Her skin sweating
Her heart racing
She lay there blindfolded as each of them
    repeatedly found use of any part of her
    they could manage to reach
The total count of the congregation had never
    been calculated
But her followers arrived en masse

She had never felt so complete
    so full
Smiling internally as she knew the result of
    every groan
    gasp and
    expletive
The fluid that was swallowed
    that landed on her skin
    that was pushed into places
    no finger or tongue could ever reach
Were nothing but
    their prayers
    their devotions
    their tithes

And all would be cherished and answered
    by their goddess in her own time

But for now the worship would continue until
    no more use could be of her
    parishioners

Then she would silently reflect under
    warm falling water as those who
    remained most devout fought to
    bathe
    wash
    and honor their deity

Warm Spring Days

Warm spring days and the
    rains they bring
    coax the trees to wake from their
    winter slumber
Budding to fill the landscape with
    colorful leaves and blooms
Much like it was the first time
    I touched her

Windowsill

Flowers were collected and kept in
    jars of water
They were hurt and dying
    unable to make their own
    sunlight or rain
She felt the same and wished for someone
    to pluck
    and place her in a warm bath
    on a bright windowsill
She wanted to be saved
She wanted it to be by him

Like a Sunset

She lowered and settled onto me as the
    sun lays on the
    late afternoon horizon
All was golden while she loved me
Bringing my release to fill her like a
    sunset to a day that was only
    ours to enjoy

Toil

My star, my sun
She floats
    ever present in the sky above me
The clouds may constantly drift between us
    bringing passing sprinkles
    and thunderstorms
But each time I wait for her light
    to return
And despite the constant toil between
    shade and sunlight
I never gaze towards a sunset
I never want summer to end

Morning Light

Her lips tasted like a sunrise
How he loved kissing them while her
    mouth was kept covered
    by a hand determined
    to help her keep quiet
When finished the movements his
    adoring mouth held
    became slow
    intermittent shudders
He left such soft skin with a simple kiss
And as they parted he could feel the shimmer
    on his face
The glistening that covered him reflected
    the light she provided
    in the same manner oceans return
    the sun's morning light

His Embrace

He always bestowed an embrace that was
    thick
    heavy and
    warm
As any proper blanket should be

And the way he filled her under bedsheets
    was a fire in a furnace that never
    left her to shiver and
    dream of warmer days
The way he loved made winters seem bearable

First Night

The first night of this cold season
She lay wrapped in sheets
    and blankets
Breathing heavily with the inclusion of the
    occasional
    adorable
    snore
How could I resist from placing silent kisses
    on the bare shoulders
        that happened to find themselves
        exposed to my affection?

Depraved

I held her hand across the table of a
    crowded restaurant
Gently stroking her with my thumb
She spoke of her day while my eyes
    gazed into hers
I could think of nothing but the
    depraved
    vile
    and
    indecent acts I would love to be sharing
    with the woman whose hand I held
All in an effort to assure that she forgot about
    the troubles of her day

Keeping That There

A smile or nod greeted so many who
    could have never known
Casually walking past multitudes of strangers
    on a day that wasn't unlike
    any other

It was earlier in the day
    in the first hours of morning
    but
    to her it seemed like seconds ago

When remembering
    she could still see him
    smell him
    taste him
The look on his face shortly after showering
The moment she pulled her head back and
    stroked his wet fucking dick
    seemed to be imprinted on
    the inside of her eyelids
Eyes watching as he gently sprayed towards her
    while a fiendish mind worked

The flat side of her first finger slid
    the reward of her toil
    toward a nipple exposed by the tugging
    of a strap with
    her left hand

She stood before he had a chance to
    catch his breath

Letting him know she was keeping "that" there
    before buttoning her blouse
    kissing his shocked smile and
    exiting the room

Last Supper

Looking down only to catch the
    lubricated shimmer
    on the skin that was repeatedly
    disappearing and reappearing
    from the offering that was
    bent over in front of him
Taking her gift in a place she had never been
    entered before
His fingertips digging into her flesh as she was
    spread open in a way
    reminiscent of the breaking of bread
    at the last supper
Indeed would he take and eat as it was known
    that her body was given to be
    broken by him
For the forgiveness of sins

Panic

The immobilizing weight of him on her back
His hands resting between shoulder blades
    as he repeatedly pushed into her
    with all of the energy within him
The pressure of her breasts being
    forced against the mattress
    was overshadowed by the fight for oxygen
    as her face found it difficult to escape
    the plush pillow that nightly caresses
    her dreaming head
At times it was a struggle to breathe
    and select gasps were sprinkled with panic
Causing a tightness around him which
    forced her to feel fuller
    than she already was
There were moments of fear but she
    never cried out
If this is what dying felt like
    why would anyone want to be alive?

Something to Covet

Standing in the doorway
    I watched her feet lift
    before her toes were introduced to
    then fully submerged into the bath
    I had drawn for her
I gazed lovingly as the skin covering her
    began to glisten as she washed herself
    in front of me
I remarked coyly about how jealous the liquid
    that could come from me was
    of the lather that rolled over her breasts
    and across stiff nipples
She smiled and signaled me with a curling finger
I approached and the blue of my jeans darkened
    as she met the zipper
    with her wet hands
Without looking away from the newly released
    flesh now held
She massaged me with handfuls of soap
    until I grew firm

She twisted
> turned and
> pulled with her grip

Making eye contact with me before proclaiming
> that she was going give the lather that
> was so recently rinsed from her skin
> something to covet

Bourbon

Bourbon flavored kisses excited her
He became relaxed
    and
       open to experimentation
       when the liquor flowed through his veins
Smiling at his gaze started her
    process of thought
She had boundaries to push

Shoulder Tap

Standing next to her
She watched for some time until deciding to
    tap her guest on the shoulder and
    motion for her to move aside
She loved the taste of another woman
    when it was on her man

Page After Page

Afternoon approached and yet
> she entered the room with nothing
> covering her skin except for a pair of
> teal panties

As she passed
> the recently purchased novel he read
> was lifted from his hands
> as she found a seat across the room

Leaning back on the brown leather sofa
> her legs spread and his new book was
> placed between them

She licked her fingers in a way one would
> before turning a page
> prior to placing them out of sight
> behind the hardback that kept her
> motions hidden

Their eyes remained locked as she turned
> page after page

Quietly telling a story that
> desperately needed told

The plot thickened and
	as the climax approached
	she tried so hard to keep a straight face
Failing of course
	to his pure delight

His Favorite Coffee

Much like his favorite coffee
She was
    aromatic
    rich and
    bold across his tongue
The mere speaking of her name in his head
    brought memories of the
    flavor he had savored
He closed his eyes and brought the cup
    to his lips
And when he sipped
The heat that gently caressed his face made
    his heart skip a beat
How he wished the warmth around his mouth
    was her

Mosaic

Elements of affection were combined
    in the sweetest of ways
He built her piece by piece
The purest of intentions were not to be
    masked by tears
    cries or
    marks and bruises shyly appearing
    on her skin
The bliss and the ache
The soreness and delight
The release granted as he assembled
    a mosaic far too holy
    to merely display in a cathedral

Terminal

Her eyes were wide
Breasts rising and falling rapidly as I
    spilled within and
    filled her
We breathed heavily together as I grew soft and
    gently slid out of her ass
A gasp accompanied her exhale as I did
With rosy cheeks and a winded smile
    her eyes locked with mine
I giggled slightly
    as I occasionally do when I cum
At that moment I knew
This was it
This was terminal

The Shadow

The shadow waited patiently at the top
    of the staircase
Each step taken echoed within a naked chest
    as the heart within began to pound
Toes slightly curled and grabbed at the
    carpet covered hardwood
    each time a foot took its turn to
    lift her closer
Approaching the summit
    a hand became extended
    silently waiting for hers
The grip his fingers held aided her final steps
When she reached the level above
    it was as though her lungs were
    taking air into them differently
The way she did when her cord was cut and
    they were forced to embrace
    that inaugural intake of oxygen
Preparing to cry out and breathe
    so much heavier

Uncommon Stout

The way his hands held the glass
Knuckles glowing in the warmly lit
    microbrewery they frequented to
    eat and drink
Eyes closing as he takes and enjoys that
    first sip

Much as he does when tasting her

She remarked silently to herself how he looked
    with the pint up to his lips
As if she was gazing over her vulva to see him
    enjoying himself

For a moment she thought about
    how it would feel
    standing
    removing the panties under her skirt
    and seating her bare ass on the booth table
    in front of him

The gasps and glares of surprised onlookers
    being seated by the hostess along with
    the faint scent of coffee
    from the remaining stout
    in his abandoned glass
    assembled the ambient cloud around them

In her mind she spread and sighed as his lips
    parted those below
    causing her to
    water a tongue whose movements
    were felt and not seen

Quenching his thirst as he
    became drunk from
    the pleasure he swallowed

Her Own Pages

So many books had been purchased
More than she would ever read
Especially when she fell infatuated
    with their stories
    and the men and women in them
So much that she would spend hours
    with their covers closed
    while licking fingers
    and
    turning her own pages

No Better Reason

For once
    he wished there was a religion
    for him to claim
Simply because there could be no
    better reason to defy a god
    than the things he thought about
    when looking at her

Those Eyes

Those eyes would weaken me
How they
    made me hungry
    made me ache
Much more than any other part of her
    ever could

Corona

The corona of her curves was clearly visible as
    she held the towel in front of her
I knew gazing upon an eclipse with naked eyes
    could cause blindness
    but
    I had no intention of looking away
If she was the last thing
    that I would remember seeing
    then so be it
I couldn't think of a more deserving
    celestial occurrence
        to which I could sacrifice my sight

Equal Parts

Without a will of her own
An autonomous
      instinctual dropping of her jaw occurred
      as his hand was placed under her chin
He was so close
She could feel his every exhale swirl through
      her open mouth

Their lips nearly touched

But unlike countless times before
      no kisses were exchanged
He spat in her mouth and gave her throat
      a firm squeeze
She was equal parts
      shocked and
      disgusted
But at the same time
      undeniably aroused when she felt
      his saliva strike her tongue

Just Fill Me

Looking down she noticed the
    closing of eyes that accompanied the
    flushing of the cheeks and chest
    below her
She repeatedly pushed onto and rose from
    her lover
Leaning towards the clinched eyelids
    of the man she loved
    she whispered sternly
"Fuck…just fill me."
He was left with no choice but to
    obey her command
Quietly grunting as he made
    the movements within
    oh so sweet and soft
    while she laid kisses to his
    trembling forehead

Breakfast in Bed

The sound of falling water stopped
Muffled footsteps and random shuffling
    were heard from the other
    side of the wall
The door opened and a waft of humidity
    preceded his entrance
She extended open hands from underneath
    the comforter that kept her warm
A smile made its way across his face
    as he approached outstretched arms
She wrapped them around him
    when he was near enough
The scent of his body wash
    flooded senses as she took him
    behind her lips
She vocalized her graciousness
    as he grew
    firm and
    long
    in her mouth
A loving tongue explored the velvety texture
    of his skin
    as warm
    freshly awakened hands massaged
    in unison with her lips

He closed his eyes to amplify the sense of touch
    before legs grew weak
    knees shuddered and
    he filled her mouth as payment for
    the pleasure she gave
All was swallowed as she continued using
    dedicated lips and fingertips
    to keep him shaking
When satisfied
    playful eyes looked up until his opened
    and connected their gaze
Her smile caused him to
    before she spoke and thanked him for
    breakfast in bed

Jigsaw

She felt so complete
It was as if she had somehow been
    solved
    and assembled
He connected the fragments
Making them tightly interlock
    in order to
    show his eyes the gorgeous image
    he was enjoying
He took in the sight of the way she had
    lifted and presented herself
As he did a smile crept across his face
    before licking his fingers
    polishing himself to a shine and
    making that final piece fit

Like Fire

Light was cast from the streetlamp
    outside the window
Raindrops clinging to the glass cast
    polka dot shadows over the bare skin
    laying next to me
I traced and connected them with the tip
    of my finger
Watching the goosebumps and raised hairs
    follow like fire along a trail of gasoline

Born Without Eyes

Even if she had been born without eyes
    she would have died
        swearing he had shown her heaven

Kissing Goodbye

Kissing her goodbye was like
    listening to the last lyric of
    my favorite song

Halo

The darkness of the room disappeared
      as she came nearer
Wings folding behind as bare feet
      stepped over the threshold of the door
The light from her halo illuminated the room
      in a way I could never
      find words to describe

She lifted arms

Gripping the shimmering circle floating
      above hair that reflected its glow
Everything around us dimmed as her
      heavenly ornament was lowered and
      offered to me in open hands
No longer a halo of light
      but a collar of leather
I accepted the gift she offered and
      closed my fingers around it

Stepping behind and standing closer than any
      could have before
      I watched her wings evaporate into the air
She lifted heavy hair to allow the fastening
      of buckles as the back of my fingers
      savored their contact with the
      skin of her neck

She breathed softly as the weight settled
    onto her shoulders
Taking a step back I watched as she knelt
    before me
She floated down like a feather falling from
    the sky to the ground
Eventually leaning forward away
    from where I stood and resting her
    forehead on the floor
Arms crawled from underneath as they extended
    and turned palms upward

It was then she spoke
"I give all of myself to you
    if only you'll be mine."

To which I replied
"I will be yours. You will be mine. The sun itself
    will set to the night we create and
    the fireflies will blink to tell generations
    of the love that we make."

An audible breath blew past her lips in
    acceptance

I then focused on her feet as they slowly found
    distance from one another

She lay there open and on display

A sight that stole my breath

Placing within my heart more joy than any
        felt by either Mary
Even as they discovered
        the stone had been rolled away
        from the entrance of their savior's
        empty tomb

My knees dropped to the floor at the revelation
        of the vision my eyes almost refused to
        believe they were seeing

I found my lips on the bottom of her right foot
Kissing a sole that had never fully been planted
        on any ground
Soft
Smooth and
Uncalloused against me

Stopping for a moment I gaze above me
Tracing this inner thigh with my line of sight and
        fixating at where her body comes together

I couldn't look away

It was almost as if I'd become caught up
        in a moment
        staring at a full moon on a
        clear winter's night

I had to taste her

And when I did
      the whole world seemed to make sense
Like every prayer I'd ever spoken was right there
      on the tip of my tongue
I held her open like frail bible pages
      and read as deeply as I possibly could
      in an effort to uncover and define
      any obscure metaphors or
      divine insight that might be otherwise
      buried in the text

No words assembled themselves as her voice
      was cast from wall to wall
Articulating
Enunciating and
Speaking into and against her caused her song
      to be broken with unexpected breaths as
      everything inside of her tried to continue
      this unintelligible singing

Craving sight but closing my eyes
      I slowly raised the efforts of my
      deciphering mouth slightly higher
As I firmly pushed to taste another of her
      internal pathways
      my fingers had to constantly remind
      themselves to never let her believe
      I was ever
      not touching her

She slowly rocked herself back and forth
    against my tongue
Her incoherent song became a pointless lullaby
    as I was seemingly already dreaming

I opened my eyes

Being careful to keep the attention of my tongue
    firmly anchored
Enthralled in a kiss so sinful that she feared
    the flames of agitated hellfire could burst
    from within her at any moment

I looked down over the valley of her arched back
Taking in the topography of the contracted
    muscles that ran parallel on each side
    of her spine
A firm
    muscular landscape that trapped the violet
    shadows of light the envious moon cast
    over her
I watched as her follicles applauded the cool air
Raising and casting
    uncountable facets of light and dark
    across rises and falls of the skin
    they extended from
At times it was almost as if they moved
Like watching the long grass of a meadow blow
    over the ground on a
    blustery day

She began to lift her head
I stared like a child taking in his first sunrise
    as the horizon of her shoulders gave way
    to a face I couldn't quite see
Her eyes tried to find mine
    to watch me taste her insides
    but the reach of her neck just would not
    allow it
This forced the sun to set once more as she
    lay her head on the floor yet again
    as my tongue gently withdrew from her

She sighed

A lament felt from bodies that had separated
    after an embrace that was surely
    never meant to end

I found myself kneeling behind and used my
    fingertips to open her
Placing these warm fingers around myself I
    stroked and manipulated the skin that
    made me a man to the sight of her
Eventually making my way
Catching the illuminated liquid that timelessly
    hung from between her legs and
    slowly massaged the fluid back into her

Releasing the grip I had upon myself
    my hands reached
        grasped and rocked her body towards me

I tensed to hold steady
Enjoying the moment as the first inch was
    cradled by her damp warmth
I drew her nearer and when our skin met
    there was fire
Not hellfire from below
    but a burning reserved for experience
    by a god determined to keep this flame
    secret from all beings but himself

I watched as palms at the floor
    closed themselves into fists
Pillars to support herself on as her movements
    began to match those of mine

My fingertips moved from the place
    on her heavenly body that has been
    held open so carefully as to allow me the
    vision of myself
    disappearing and reappearing
    coated in the shimmer of her
They crawled as slowly as ivy
Finding places to stand between stones
    on forgotten walls

Moving past marks of the two places on
    untouched skin
        that once held her wings
Scars that faded as my touch removed
    and brushed any traces of them away
        like a mistake erased from
        a piece of paper

Eventually finding shoulders before wandering
    toward her neck
Their vines intertwined around her throat as
    I pulled tightly and senselessly tried
    to compress our bodies into a single being

I couldn't help but spill inside of her
Holding tightly as she felt my pulse pounding
    within
A delightful tempo
A near tickling underneath unexplored flesh
    that had until this moment
    never felt a heartbeat of its own

The groans came from my mouth but I felt them
    shake under the grip I had on the
    vessel that contained her voice

Fingers released and slowly found their way
    down her back like rain
Puddles in the form of my hands held her
    open wide once again

As I slid from her and an unspoken loneliness
    began to creep around our hearts
I caught what dripped from her in
    an eager palm

She spilled onto the floor
Resting on her side as I crept up and
    at last
    joined her eyes with mine
I brought my filled hand to her lips
    and she extended a tongue
    tasted and
    drank the water of us
My own mouth approached and savored
    along with hers as
    this was an elixir
    meant to be enjoyed together

Our tongues met in an embrace wrapped in the
    warm blanket of our mouths and
    the taste of what was
    her inaugural sin

She rested a weary head upon the floor
Feeling like she had been flying despite knowing
    that her wings were gone
Feeling like she was so much more an angel now
    than she had ever been before
    despite words
    from the holy one telling her she was

Her eyes sparkled as I held her head in my
	hands
		laying her to relax in the pillow of my palm

She whispered
"Eloi, eloi, lema sabachthani?"

I shushed her as my fingers ran through her hair
Letting her know that she would be my treasure
		and would never be forsaken again

Applause

We danced barefoot in the grass as the
    moon sat high
Arms entangled
Lips planted so that tongues could
    taste the salty sweat of summer skin
Bodies starved for one another
    as her breasts were compressed
    tightly against me by the
    strength of my embrace
Fireflies drifted around us in swarms
Signaling and blowing chartreuse kisses
    to the delight of their lovers
    who adored them from the ground
She was mine
They were theirs
And we all turned and twirled to the
    applause of century-old trees
    smiling at the sight of our young love

Thank you.

I would personally like to thank everyone for their support, help and encouragement with this project by name, but we don't have that kind of time. Please know that every drop of support or encouragement, no matter how small, is taken to heart and appreciated. I will express my gratitude to Alex for the beautiful cover art, and to Brooke for correcting my mistakes.

This is for Sara. Without you, life wouldn't be the same. Thank you for loving me, supporting me and dealing with my ridiculousness on a daily basis. Kissing you before I leave and when I arrive home is the sunrise and sunset to my day. Having your arms around me brightens any cloudy sky. I love you, my dear.

Made in the USA
Las Vegas, NV
30 October 2023